SECRETS OF THE LIBRARY OF DOOM

INVISIBLE INK

BY MICHAEL DAHL

ILLUSTRATED BY PATRICIO CLAREY

Raintree is an imprint of Capstone Global Library Limited, a company
incorporated in England and Wales having its registered office at 264
Banbury Road, Oxford, OX2 7DY – Registered company number: 6695582

www.raintree.co.uk
myorders@raintree.co.uk

Designed by Hilary Wacholz
Original illustrations © Capstone Global Library Limited 2021
Originated by Capstone Global Library Ltd

978 1 3982 0327 3

British Library Cataloguing in Publication Data
A full catalogue record for this book is available from the British Library.

CONTENTS

The Library of Doom is a hidden fortress.
It holds the world's largest collection
of strange and dangerous books.

Behold the Librarian. He defends the Library – and
the world – from super-villains, clever thieves,
and fierce monsters. Many of his adventures
have remained secret. Now they can be told.

SECRET #99
YOU DON'T ALWAYS HAVE TO SEE
SOMETHING TO KNOW IT'S THERE.

Chapter One

INVISIBLE INC.

Night covers the city. Wind **BLOWS** through the dark alleys.

The FULL moon above the city is as blank as an empty page.

In one alley, the wind STIRS up dead leaves. They skitter in front of a small building.

The windows are **DARK**.

A sign hangs above the door. It reads:

INVISIBLE INC.

The sign **SWINGS** back and forth,
creaking.

REAKKK REAKKK REEAAAKKKK!

The door to the building suddenly
opens.

A strange man steps out.

His hair is wild. His eyes are hidden by **THICK** glasses.

REAKKK REAKKK REEAAAKKKK!

The man glances up at the noisy sign.

Then he pulls something from his coat. It is a weird SPRAY bottle.

The man aims the bottle at the sign.
He sprays a thick green **GAS**.

The **GAS** wraps around the sign.

The words on the sign begin to fade. Soon, they are gone.

"Invisible Inc. is now invisible ink," whispers the man.

He hides the bottle back in his coat. Then he hurries down the **ALLEY**.

Chapter Two

THE HEAD IN THE WINDOW

Not far away, a young man **LOOKS** through a shop window.

"That's it!" he says to himself. "There is *The Floating Head*!"

The young man **RUSHES** into the bookshop.

Piles of OLD books cover the floor. More books fill the shelves.

The young man turns to the main window. He reaches out to grab *The Floating Head*.

"AAAHHHHH!" he screams.

A head with WILD hair is floating in the darkness outside. It is staring at him.

The door to the bookshop opens.

A strange man with WILD hair steps inside.

The stranger looks at the young man. He gives a wide SMILE.

"I hope I did not **SCARE** you," the stranger says.

The young man **SHRUGS**. "It was nothing," he says.

The young man hands his book to the shop assistant. He pulls out several notes and hands them to her too.

"You are right," says the stranger. "It *is* nothing!"

Chapter Three

GONE OR INVISIBLE?

The stranger pulls out a weird bottle. He aims it into the shop and **SPRAYS**.

FFFSSSSSSSSHHHHHHH!

A thick green GAS covers the books and the people.

When the GAS clears, the stranger is gone.

"What was that all about?" asks the young man. He COUGHS as he grabs his book.

"Wait a minute," says the assistant. "The ink has disappeared from your money! These notes are just blank paper!"

The young man **FLIPS** through his book. "All the pages are empty!" he says.

Chapter Four

PURPLE GAS

A woman **SCREAMS** outside the bookshop

The young man rushes into the **ALLEY**.

"My bike!" the woman shouts.
"Someone **STOLE** the number plates!"

The strange man with the SPRAY bottle stands nearby. He smiles.

"They are still there," the man says. "Only now the numbers and letters are invisible!"

The young man looks at the road sign on the corner. "The sign is blank too," he whispers.

The woman stares at something else.
"Is that a man in the sky?" she asks.

The stranger quickly looks up. "No!" he
SCREAMS into the sky. "You can't stop
me, Librarian!"

The flying LIBRARIAN lands
in the alley. A street light shines off his
dark glasses.

The Librarian points at the stranger. "Give up, Eraser," he says. "Your plan to **DESTROY** all books won't work."

The WILD-haired Eraser shouts, "That's what you think! When I find your Library, your books will be truly doomed!"

The Eraser pushes a hidden button on his bottle. A huge cloud of purple GAS sprays out.

The **GAS** wraps around the Librarian.

"Now *you're* invisible," the Eraser laughs.

Chapter Five

BLINDED BY THE LIGHT

The purple **GAS** clears. The Librarian is gone. Only his glasses can be seen hanging in the air.

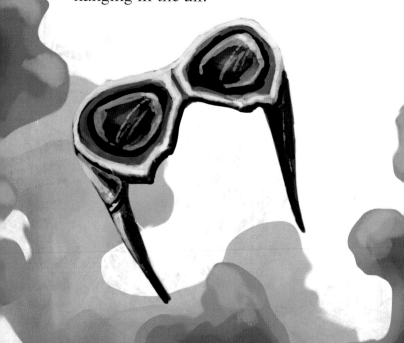

The Librarian's voice **ECHOES** through the alley. "Here's some *light* reading!" he says.

The light shining off the Librarian's glasses grows brighter. And brighter.

Light **BURSTS** out from the glasses like rays of sunlight.

ZZZZZZZZZSSSSSSSS!!!!

The light **BURNS** into the motorcycle's number plates. It blasts the road sign.

Light blazes into the bookshop's windows.

"My books!" the assistant **SHOUTS** from inside the shop. "All the words are <u>back</u> in my books!"

The blinding light fades away.

The alley is **DARK** again. But the number plates and the road sign are back to normal.

The light brought back all the **MISSING** letters and words.

The LIBRARIAN is back too. He holds the Eraser's shoulder.

"I can't move!" yells the Eraser. "It feels like a CHAIN is wrapped around me!"

"Yes, it is an invisible chain," says the Librarian. "Or, you might call them *invisible links*."

FWWWWOOOOSHHH!

The Librarian **FLIES** back into the air
with the Eraser.

The young man looks down at the cover of *The Floating Head*.

Then he looks up at the hero. "Now *he* should be in a book!" he says.

GLOSSARY

alley small path between buildings

assistant someone who works in a shop

blaze shine brightly

disappear pass out of sight

glance look quickly at something

inc. short for the word *incorporated*; it is part of the name of many companies

invisible not possible to see

links small metal loops that make up a chain

weird very strange and not normal

TALK ABOUT IT

1. The story takes place at night. What feeling does that create? How would the story be different if it took place during the day?

2. How would you describe the Eraser? How does he behave? What is his goal? Use examples to support your answer.

WRITE ABOUT IT

1. Imagine if all the ink in your school and home became invisible. Write a paragraph about how life would be different. Write a story about how you return everything to normal.

2. The Eraser has a green gas that makes ink invisible and a purple gas that makes people disappear. What other types of gas might be in the bottle? Write about what they do.

ABOUT THE AUTHOR

Michael Dahl is an award-winning author of more than 200 books for young people. He especially likes to write scary or weird fiction. His latest series are the sci-fi adventure Escape from Planet Alcatraz and School Bus of Horrors. As a child, he spent lots of time in libraries. "The creepier, the better," he says. These days, besides writing, he likes travelling and hunting for the one, true door that leads to the Library of Doom.

ABOUT THE ILLUSTRATOR

Patricio Clarey was born in 1978 in Argentina. He graduated in fine arts from the Martín A. Malharro School of Visual Arts, specializing in illustration and graphic design. Patricio currently lives in Barcelona, Spain, where he works as a freelance graphic designer and illustrator. He has created several comics and graphic novels, and his work has been featured in books and other publications.